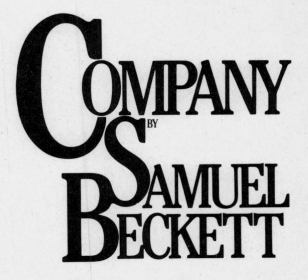

COMPANY

BY

SAMUEL BECKETT

Grove Press, Inc., New York

First Edition 1980
Second Printing 1981
ISBN: 0-394-51394-0
Library of Congress Catalog Card Number: 80-995

First Evergreen Edition 1981
First Printing 1981
ISBN: 0-394-17928-5
Library of Congress Catalog Card Number: 80-995

Library of Congress Cataloging in Publication Data

Beckett, Samuel, 1906–
Company.

I.   Title.
PR6003. E282C65 1980   822'.912   80-995
ISBN 0-394-51394-0
ISBN 0-394-17928-5 pbk

Manufactured in the United States of America

GROVE PRESS INC., 196 West Houston Street,
New York, N.Y. 10014

COMPANY

A voice comes to one in the dark. Imagine.

To one on his back in the dark. This he can tell by the pressure on his hind parts and by how the dark changes when he shuts his eyes and again when he opens them again. Only a small part of what is said can be verified. As for example when he hears, You are on your back in the dark. Then he must acknowledge the truth of what is said. But by far the greater part of what is said cannot be verified. As for example when he hears, You first saw the light on such and such a day. Sometimes the two are combined as for example, You first saw the light on such and such a day and now you are on your back in the dark. A device perhaps from the incontrovertibility of the one to win credence for the other. That then is the proposition. To one on his back in the dark a voice tells of a past. With occasional allusion to a present and more rarely to a future as for example, You will end as you now are. And in another dark or in the same another devising it all for company. Quick leave him.

Use of the second person marks the voice. That of the third that cankerous other. Could he speak to and of whom the voice speaks there would be a first. But he cannot. He shall not. You cannot. You shall not.

Apart from the voice and the faint sound of his breath there is no sound. None at least that he can hear. This he can tell by the faint sound of his breath.

Though now even less than ever given to wonder he cannot but sometimes wonder if it is indeed to and of him the voice is speaking. May not there be another with him in the dark to and of whom the voice is speaking? Is he not perhaps overhearing a communication not intended for him? If he is alone on his back in the dark why does the voice not say so? Why does it never say for example, You saw the light on such and such a day and now you are alone on your back in the dark? Why? Perhaps for no other reason than to kindle in his mind this faint uncertainty and embarrassment.

Your mind never active at any time is now even less than ever so. This is the type of assertion he does not question. You saw the light on such and such a day and your mind never active at any time is now even less than ever so. Yet a certain activity of mind however slight is a necessary adjunct of company. That is why the voice does not say, You are on your back in the dark and have no mental activity of any kind. The voice alone is company but not enough. Its effect on the hearer is a necessary complement. Were it only to kindle in his mind the state of faint uncertainty and embarrassment mentioned above. But company apart this effect is clearly necessary. For were he merely to hear the voice and it to have no more effect on him than speech in Bantu or in Erse then might it not as well cease? Unless its object be by mere sound to plague one in need of silence. Or of course unless as above surmised directed at another.

A small boy you come out of Connolly's Stores holding your mother by the hand. You turn right and advance in silence southward along the highway. After some hundred paces you head inland and broach the long steep homeward. You make ground in silence hand in hand through the warm still summer air. It is late afternoon and after some hundred paces the sun appears above the crest of the rise. Looking up at the blue sky and then at your mother's face you break the silence asking her if it is not in reality much more distant than it appears. The sky that is. The blue sky. Receiving no answer you mentally reframe your question and some hundred paces later look up at her face again and ask her if it does not appear much less distant than in reality it is. For some reason you could never fathom this question must have angered her exceedingly. For she shook off your little hand and made you a cutting retort you have never forgotten.

If the voice is not speaking to him it must be speaking to another. So with what reason remains he reasons. To another of that other. Or of him. Or of another still. To another of that other or of him or of another still. To one on his back in the dark in any case. Of one on his back in the dark whether the same or another. So with what reason remains he reasons and reasons ill. For were the voice speaking not to him but to another then it must be of that other it is speaking and not of him or of another still. Since it speaks in the second person. Were it not of him to whom it is speaking speaking but of another it would not speak in the second person but in the third. For example, He first saw the light on such and such a day and now he is on his back in the dark. It is clear therefore that if it is not to him the voice is speaking but to another it is not of him either but of that other and none other to that other. So with what reason remains he reasons ill. In order to be company he must display a certain mental activity. But it need not be of a high order. Indeed it might be argued the lower the better. Up to a point. The lower the order of mental activity the better the company. Up to a point.

You first saw the light in the room you most likely were conceived in. The big bow window looked west to the mountain. Mainly west. For being bow it looked also a little south and a little north. Necessarily. A little south to more mountain and a little north to foot-hill and plain. The midwife was none other than a Dr Hadden or Haddon. Straggling grey moustache and hunted look. It being a public holiday your father left the house soon after his breakfast with a flask and a package of his favourite egg sandwiches for a tramp in the mountains. There was nothing unusual in this. But on that particular morning his love of walking and wild scenery was not the only mover. But he was moved also to take himself off and out of the way by his aver-sion to the pains and general unpleasant-ness of labour and delivery. Hence the sandwiches which he relished at noon looking out to sea from the lee of a great rock on the first summit scaled. You may imagine his thoughts before and after as he strode through the gorse and heather. When he returned at nightfall he learned to his dismay from the maid at the back door that labour was still in swing. Despite its having begun before he left the house full ten hours earlier. He at once hastened to the coachhouse some twenty yards distant where he housed his De Dion Bouton. He shut the doors behind him and climbed into the driver's seat. You may imagine his thoughts as he sat there in the dark not knowing what to think. Though footsore and weary he was on the point of setting out anew across the fields in the young moonlight when the maid came running to tell him it was over at last. Over!

You are an old man plodding along a narrow country road. You have been out since break of day and now it is evening. Sole sound in the silence your footfalls. Rather sole sounds for they vary from one to the next. You listen to each one and add it in your mind to the growing sum of those that went before. You halt with bowed head on the

verge of the ditch and convert into yards.
On the basis now of two steps per yard. So
many since dawn to add to yesterday's. To
yesteryear's. To yesteryears'. Days other
than today and so akin. The giant tot in
miles. In leagues. How often round the
earth already. Halted too at your elbow
during these computations your father's
shade. In his old tramping rags. Finally on
side by side from nought anew.

The voice comes to him
now from one quarter and now from another. Now faint from afar and now a
murmur in his ear. In the course of a single sentence it may change place and tone.
Thus for example clear from above his upturned face, You first saw the light at
Easter and now. Then a murmur in his
ear, You are on your back in the dark. Or
of course vice versa. Another trait its long
silences when he dare almost hope it is at
an end. Thus to take the same example
clear from above his upturned face, You

first saw the light of day the day Christ
died and now. Then long after on his nas-
cent hope the murmur, You are on your
back in the dark. Or of course vice versa.

Another trait its repeti-
tiousness. Repeatedly with only minor
variants the same bygone. As if willing
him by this dint to make it his. To confess,
Yes I remember. Perhaps even to have a
voice. To murmur, Yes I remember. What
an addition to company that would be! A
voice in the first person singular. Mur-
muring now and then, Yes I remember.

An old beggar woman is
fumbling at a big garden gate. Half blind.
You know the place well. Stone deaf and
not in her right mind the woman of the
house is a crony of your mother. She was
sure she could fly once in the air. So one
day she launched herself from a first floor
window. On the way home from kinder-

garten on your tiny cycle you see the poor old beggar woman trying to get in. You dismount and open the gate for her. She blesses you. What were her words? God reward you little master. Some such words. God save you little master.

A faint voice at loudest. It slowly ebbs till almost out of hearing. Then slowly back to faint full. At each slow ebb hope slowly dawns that it is dying. He must know it will flow again. And yet at each slow ebb hope slowly dawns that it is dying.

Slowly he entered dark and silence and lay there for so long that with what judgement remained he judged them to be final. Till one day the voice. One day! Till in the end the voice saying, You are on your back in the dark. Those its first words. Long pause for him to be-lieve his ears and then from another quarter the same. Next the vow not to cease till hearing cease. You are on your back in the dark and not till hearing cease will this voice cease. Or another way. As in shadow he lay and only the odd sound slowly silence fell and darkness gathered. That were perhaps better company. For what odd sound? Whence the shadowy light?

You stand at the tip of the high board. High above the sea. In it your father's upturned face. Upturned to you. You look down to the loved trusted face. He calls to you to jump. He calls, Be a brave boy. The red round face. The thick moustache. The greying hair. The swell sways it under and sways it up again. The far call again, Be a brave boy. Many eyes upon you. From the water and from the bathing place.

The odd sound. What a mercy to have that to turn to. Now and then. In dark and silence to close as if to light the eyes and hear a sound. Some object moving from its place to its last place. Some soft thing softly stirring soon to stir no more. To darkness visible to close the eyes and hear if only that. Some soft thing softly stirring soon to stir no more.

By the voice a faint light is shed. Dark lightens while it sounds. Deepens when it ebbs. Lightens with flow back to faint full. Is whole again when it ceases. You are on your back in the dark. Had the eyes been open then they would have marked a change.

Whence the shadowy light? What company in the dark! To close the eyes and try to imagine that. Whence once the shadowy light. No source. As if faintly luminous all his little void. What can he have seen then above his upturned face. To close the eyes in the dark and try to imagine that.

Another trait the flat tone. No life. Same flat tone at all times. For its affirmations. For its negations. For its interrogations. For its exclamations. For its imperations. Same flat tone. You were once. You were never. Were you ever? Oh never to have been! Be again. Same flat tone.

Can he move? Does he move? Should he move? What a help that would be. When the voice fails. Some movement however small. Were it but of a hand closing. Or opening if closed to begin. What a help that would be in the dark! To close the eyes and see that hand. Palm upward filling the whole field. The lines. The fingers slowly down. Or up if down to begin. The lines of that old palm.

There is of course the eye. Filling the whole field. The hood slowly down. Or up if down to begin. The globe. All pupil. Staring up. Hooded. Bared. Hooded again. Bared again.

If he were to utter after all? However feebly. What an addition to company that would be! You are on your back in the dark and one day you will utter again. One day! In the end. In the end you will utter again. Yes I remember. That was I. That was I then.

You are alone in the garden. Your mother is in the kitchen making ready for afternoon tea with Mrs. Coote. Making the wafer-thin bread and butter. From behind a bush you watch Mrs Coote arrive. A small thin sour woman. Your mother answers her saying, He is playing in the garden. You climb to near the top of a great fir. You sit a little listening to all the sounds. Then throw yourself off. The great boughs break your fall. The needles. You lie a little with your face to the ground. Then climb the tree again. Your mother answers Mrs Coote again saying, He has been a very naughty boy.

What with what feeling remains does he feel about now as compared to then? When with what judgement remained he judged his condition final. As well inquire what he felt then about then as compared to before. When he still moved or tarried in remains of light. As then there was no then so there is none now.

In another dark or in the same another devising it all for company. This at first sight seems clear. But as the eye dwells it grows obscure. Indeed the longer the eye dwells the obscurer it grows. Till the eye closes and freed from pore the mind inquires, What does this mean? What finally does this mean that at first sight seemed clear? Till it the mind too closes as it were. As the window might close of a dark empty room. The single window giving on outer dark. Then nothing more. No. Unhappily no. Pangs of faint light and stirrings still. Unformulable gropings of the mind. Unstillable.

Nowhere in particular on the way from A to Z. Or say for verisimilitude the Ballyogan Road. That dear old back road. Somewhere on the Ballyogan Road in lieu of nowhere in particular. Where no truck any more. Somewhere on the Ballyogan Road on the way from A to Z. Head sunk totting up the tally on the verge of the ditch. Foothills to left. Croker's Acres ahead. Father's shade to right and a little to the rear. So many times already round the earth. Topcoat once green stiff with age and grime from chin to insteps. Battered once buff block hat and quarter boots still a match. No other garments if any to be seen. Out since break of day and night now falling. Reckoning ended on together from nought anew. As if bound for Stepaside. When suddenly you cut through the hedge and vanish hobbling east across the gallops.

For why or? Why in another dark or in the same? And whose voice asking this? Who asks, Whose voice asking this? And answers, His soever who devises it all. In the same dark as his creature or in another. For company. Who asks in the end, Who asks? And in the end answers as above? And adds long after to himself, Unless another still. Nowhere to be found. Nowhere to be sought. The unthinkable last of all. Unnamable. Last person. I. Quick leave him.

The light there was then. On your back in the dark the light there was then. Sunless cloudless brightness. You slip away at break of day and climb to your hiding place on the hillside. A nook in the gorse. East beyond the sea the faint shape of high mountain. Seventy miles away according to your Longman. For the third or fourth time in your life. The first time you told them and were derided. All you had seen was cloud. So now you hoard it in your heart with the rest. Back home at nightfall supperless to bed. You lie in the dark and are back in that light. Straining out from your nest in the gorse with your eyes across the water till they ache. You close them while you count a hundred. Then open and strain again. Again and again. Till in the end it is there. Palest blue against the pale sky. You lie in the dark and are back in that light. Fall asleep in that sunless cloudless light. Sleep till morning light.

Deviser of the voice and of its hearer and of himself. Deviser of himself for company. Leave it at that. He speaks of himself as of another. He says speaking of himself, He speaks of himself as of another. Himself he devises too for company. Leave it at that. Confusion too is company up to a point. Better hope deferred than none. Up to a point. Till the heart starts to sicken. Company too up to a point. Better a sick heart than none. Till it starts to break. So speaking of himself he concludes for the time being, For the time being leave it at that.

In the same dark as his creature or in another not yet imagined. Nor in what position. Whether standing or sitting or lying or in some other position in the dark. These are among the matters yet to be imagined. Matters of which as yet no inkling. The test is company. Which of the two darks is the better

company. Which of all imaginable posi-
tions has the most to offer in the way of
company. And similarly for the other matters yet to be imagined. Such as if such
decisions irreversible. Let him for example
after due imagination decide in favour of
the supine position or prone and this in
practice prove less companionable than
anticipated. May he then or may he not
replace it by another? Such as huddled
with his legs drawn up within the semi-
circle of his arms and his head on his
knees. Or in motion. Crawling on all
fours. Another in another dark or in the
same crawling on all fours devising it all
for company. Or some other form of motion. The possible encounters. A dead rat.
What an addition to company that would
be! A rat long dead.

Might not the hearer be
improved? Made more companionable if
not downright human. Mentally perhaps

there is room for enlivenment. An attempt at reflexion at least. At recall. At speech even. Conation of some kind however feeble. A trace of emotion. Signs of distress. A sense of failure. Without loss of character. Delicate ground. But physically? Must he lie inert to the end? Only the eyelids stirring on and off since technically they must. To let in and shut out the dark. Might he not cross his feet? On and off. Now left on right and now a little later the reverse. No. Quite out of keeping. He lie with crossed feet? One glance dispels. Some movement of the hands? A hand. A clenching and unclenching. Difficult to justify. Or raised to brush away a fly. But there are no flies. Then why not let there be? The temptation is great. Let there be a fly. For him to brush away. A live fly mistaking him for dead. Made aware of its error and renewing it incontinent. What an addition to company that would be! A live fly mistaking him for dead. But no. He would not brush away a fly.

You take pity on a hedgehog out in the cold and put it in an old hatbox with some worms. This box with the hog inside you then place in a disused hutch wedging the door open for the poor creature to come and go at will. To go in search of food and having eaten to regain the warmth and security of its box in the hutch. There then is the hedgehog in its box in the hutch with enough worms to tide it over. A last look to make sure all is as it should be before taking yourself off to look for something else to pass the time heavy already on your hands at that tender age. The glow at your good deed is slower than usual to cool and fade. You glowed readily in those days but seldom for long. Hardly had the glow been kindled by some good deed on your part or by some little triumph over your rivals or by a word of praise from your parents or mentors when it would begin to cool and fade leaving you in a very short time as chill and dim as before. Even in those days. But not this day. It was on an au-

tumn afternoon you found the hedgehog
and took pity on it in the way described
and you were still the better for it when
your bedtime came. Kneeling at your bed-
side you included it the hedgehog in your
detailed prayer to God to bless all you
loved. And tossing in your warm bed
waiting for sleep to come you were still
faintly glowing at the thought of what a
fortunate hedgehog it was to have crossed
your path as it did. A narrow clay path
edged with sere box edging. As you stood
there wondering how best to pass the time
till bedtime it parted the edging on the
one side and was making straight for the
edging on the other when you entered its
life. Now the next morning not only was
the glow spent but a great uneasiness had
taken its place. A suspicion that all was
perhaps not as it should be. That rather
than do as you did you had perhaps better
let good alone and the hedgehog pursue
its way. Days if not weeks passed before
you could bring yourself to return to the
hutch. You have never forgotten what

you found then. You are on your back in the dark and have never forgotten what you found then. The mush. The stench.

Impending for some time the following. Need for company not continuous. Moments when his own unrelieved a relief. Intrusion of voice at such. Similarly image of hearer. Similarly his own. Regret then at having brought them about and problem how dispel them. Finally what meant by his own unrelieved? What possible relief? Leave it at that for the moment.

Let the hearer be named H. Aspirate. Haitch. You Haitch are on your back in the dark. And let him know his name. No longer any question of his overhearing. Of his not being meant. Though logically none in any case. Of words murmured in his ear to wonder if to him! So he is. So that faint uneasiness

lost. That faint hope. To one with so few
occasions to feel. So inapt to feel. Asking
nothing better in so far as he can ask anything than to feel nothing. Is it desirable?
No. Would he gain thereby in compan-
ionability? No. Then let him not be
named H. Let him be again as he was. The
hearer. Unnamable. You.

Imagine closer the place
where he lies. Within reason. To its form
and dimensions a clue is given by the
voice afar. Receding afar or there with
abrupt saltation or resuming there after
pause. From above and from all sides and
levels with equal remoteness at its most
remote. At no time from below. So far.
Suggesting one lying on the floor of a
hemispherical chamber of generous diam-
eter with ear dead centre. How generous?
Given faintness of voice at its least faint
some sixty feet should suffice or thirty
from ear to any given point of encompass-

ing surface. So much for form and dimensions. And composition? What and where clue to that if any anywhere. Reserve for the moment. Basalt is tempting. Black basalt. But reserve for the moment. So he imagines to himself as voice and hearer pall. But further imagination shows him to have imagined ill. For with what right affirm of a faint sound that it is a less faint made fainter by farness and not a true faint near at hand? Or of a faint fading to fainter that it recedes and not in situ decreases. If with none then no light from the voice on the place where our old hearer lies. In immeasurable dark. Contourless. Leave it at that for the moment. Adding only, What kind of imagination is this so reason-ridden? A kind of its own.

Another devising it all for company. In the same dark as his creature or in another. Quick imagine. The same.

Might not the voice be improved? Made more companionable. Say changing now for some time past though no tense in the dark in that dim mind. All at once over and in train and to come. But for the other say for some time past some improvement. Same flat tone as initially imagined and same repetitiousness. No improving those. But less mobility. Less variety of faintness. As if seeking optimum position. From which to discharge with greatest effect. The ideal amplitude for effortless audition. Neither offending the ear with loudness nor through converse excess constraining it to strain. How far more companionable such an organ than it initially in haste imagined. How more likely to achieve its object. To have the hearer have a past and acknowledge it. You were born on an Easter Friday after long labour. Yes I remember. The sun had not long sunk behind the larches. Yes I remember. As best to erode the drop must strike unwavering. Upon the place beneath.

The last time you went out the snow lay on the ground. You now on your back in the dark stand that morning on the sill having pulled the door gently to behind you. You lean back against the door with bowed head making ready to set out. By the time you open your eyes your feet have disappeared and the skirts of your greatcoat come to rest on the surface of the snow. The dark scene seems lit from below. You see yourself at that last outset leaning against the door with closed eyes waiting for the word from you to go. To be gone. Then the snowlit scene. You lie in the dark with closed eyes and see yourself there as described making ready to strike out and away across the expanse of light. You hear again the click of the door pulled gently to and the silence before the steps can start. Next thing you are on your way across the white pasture afrolic with lambs in spring and strewn with red placentae. You take the course you always take which is a beeline for the gap or ragged

point in the quickset that forms the west-
ern fringe. Thither from your entering the
pasture you need normally from eighteen
hundred to two thousand paces depend-
ing on your humour and the state of the
ground. But on this last morning many
more will be required. Many many more.
The beeline is so familiar to your feet that
if necessary they could keep to it and you
sightless with error on arrival of not more
than a few feet north or south. And indeed without any such necessity unless
from within this is what they normally do
and not only here. For you advance if not
with closed eyes though this as often as
not at least with them fixed on the mo-
mentary ground before your feet. That is
all of nature you have seen. Since finally
you bowed your head. The fleeting
ground before your feet. From time to
time. You do not count your steps any
more. For the simple reason they number
each day the same. Average day in day out
the same. The way being always the same.
You keep count of the days and every

tenth day multiply. And add. Your father's shade is not with you any more. It fell out long ago. You do not hear your footfalls any more. Unhearing unseeing you go your way. Day after day. The same way. As if there were no other any more. For you there is no other any more. You used never to halt except to make your reckoning. So as to plod on from nought anew. This need removed as we have seen there is none in theory to halt any more. Save perhaps a moment at the outermost point. To gather yourself together for the return. And yet you do. As never before. Not for tiredness. You are no more tired now than you always were. Not because of age. You are no older now than you always were. And yet you halt as never before. So that the same hundred yards you used to cover in a matter of three to four minutes may now take you anything from fifteen to twenty. The foot falls unbidden in midstep or next for lift cleaves to the ground bringing the body to a stand. Then a speechlessness whereof the gist,

Can they go on? Or better, Shall they go on? The barest gist. Stilled when finally as always hitherto they do. You lie in the dark with closed eyes and see the scene. As you could not at the time. The dark cope of sky. The dazzling land. You at a standstill in the midst. The quarter boots sunk to the tops. The skirts of the greatcoat resting on the snow. In the old bowed head in the old block hat speechless misgiving. Halfway across the pasture on your beeline to the gap. The unerring feet fast. You look behind you as you could not then and see their trail. A great swerve. Withershins. Almost as if all at once the heart too heavy. In the end too heavy.

Bloom of adulthood. Imagine a whiff of that. On your back in the dark you remember. Ah you you remember. Cloudless May day. She joins you in the little summerhouse. A rustic hexahedron. Entirely of logs. Both larch and fir. Six feet across. Eight from floor to vertex. Area twenty-four square feet to furthest decimal. Two small multicoloured lights vis-à-vis. Small stained diamond panes. Under each a ledge. There on summer Sundays after his midday meal your father loved to retreat with *Punch* and a cushion. The waist of his trousers unbuttoned he sat on the one ledge turning the pages. You on the other with your feet dangling. When he chuckled you tried to chuckle too. When his chuckle died yours too. That you should try to imitate his chuckle pleased and tickled him greatly and sometimes he would chuckle for no other reason than to hear you try to chuckle too. Sometimes you turn your head and look out through a rose-red pane. You press your little nose against the pane and all without is rosy. The years have flown and there at the same place as then you sit in the bloom of adulthood bathed in rainbow light gazing before you. She is late. You close your eyes and try to calculate the volume. Simple sums you find a help in times of trouble. A haven. You arrive in the end at seven cubic yards approximately. Even still in the timeless dark you find figures a comfort. You assume a certain heart rate and reckon how many thumps a day. A week. A month. A year. And assuming a certain lifetime a lifetime. Till the last thump. But for the moment with hardly more than seventy American billion behind you you sit in the little summerhouse working out the volume. Seven cubic yards approximately. This strikes you for some reason as improbable and you set about your sum anew. But you have not made much headway when her light step is heard. Light for a woman of her size. You open with quickening pulse your eyes and a moment later that seems an eternity her face appears at the window. Mainly blue in this position the natural pallor you so admire as indeed from it no doubt wholly blue your own. For natural pallor is a property you have in common. The violet lips do not return your smile. Now this window being flush with your eyes from where you sit and the floor as near as no matter with the outer ground you cannot but wonder if she has not sunk to her knees. Knowing from experience that the height or length you have in common is the sum of equal segments. For when bolt upright or lying at full stretch you cleave face to face then your knees meet and your pubes and the hairs of your heads mingle. Does it follow from this that the loss of height for the body that sits is the same as for it that kneels? At this point assuming height of seat adjustable as in the case of certain piano stools you close your eyes the better with mental measure to measure and compare the first and second segments namely from sole to knee-pad and thence to pelvic girdle. How given you were both moving and at rest to the closed eye in your waking hours! By day and by night. To that perfect dark. That shadowless light. Simply to be gone. Or for affair as now. A single leg appears. Seen from above. You separate the segments and lay

them side by side. It is as you half surmised. The upper is the longer and the
sitter's loss the greater when seat at knee
level. You leave the pieces lying there and
open your eyes to find her sitting before
you. All dead still. The ruby lips do not
return your smile. Your gaze descends to
the breasts. You do not remember them so
big. To the abdomen. Same impression.
Dissolve to your father's straining against
the unbuttoned waistband. Can it be she
is with child without your having asked
for as much as her hand? You go back into
your mind. She too did you but know it
has closed her eyes. So you sit face to face
in the little summer-house. With eyes
closed and your hands on your pubes. In
that rainbow light. That dead still.

Wearied by such stretch
of imagining he ceases and all ceases. Till
feeling the need for company again he
tells himself to call the hearer M at least.
For readier reference. Himself some other

character. W. Devising it all himself included for company. In the same dark as M when last heard of. In what posture and whether fixed or mobile left open. He says further to himself referring to himself, When last he referred to himself it was to say he was in the same dark as his creature. Not in another as once seemed possible. The same. As more companionable. And that his posture there remained to be devised. And to be decided whether fast or mobile. Which of all imaginable postures least liable to pall? Which of motion or of rest the more entertaining in the long run? And in the same breath too soon to say and why after all not say without further ado what can later be unsaid and what if it could not? What then? Could he now if he chose move out of the dark he chose when last heard of and away from his creature into another? Should he now decide to lie and come later to regret it could he then rise to his feet for example and lean against a wall or pace to and fro? Could M be reimagined in an easy chair? With hands free to go to his assistance? There in the same dark as his creature he leaves himself to these perplexities while wondering as every now and then he wonders in the back of his mind if the woes of the world are all they used to be. In his day.

M so far as follows. On his back in a dark place form and dimensions yet to be devised. Hearing on and off a voice of which uncertain whether addressed to him or to another sharing his situation. There being nothing to show when it describes correctly his situation that the description is not for the benefit of another in the same situation. Vague distress at the vague thought of his perhaps overhearing a confidence when he hears for example, You are on your back in the dark. Doubts gradually dashed as voice from questing far and wide closes in upon him. When it ceases no other sound than his breath. When it ceases long enough vague hope it may have said its last. Mental activity of a low order. Rare flickers of reasoning of no avail. Hope and despair and suchlike barely felt. How current situation arrived at unclear. No that then to compare to this now. Only eyelids move. When for relief from outer and inner dark they close and open respectively. Other small local movements eventually within moderation not to be despaired of. But no improvement by means of such achieved so far. Or on a higher plane by such addition to company as a movement of sustained sorrow or desire or remorse or curiosity or anger and so on. Or by some successful act of intellection as were he to think to himself referring to himself, Since he cannot think he will give up trying. Is there anything to add to this esquisse? His unnamability. Even M must go. So W reminds himself of his creature as so far created. W? But W too is creature. Figment.

Yet another then. Of whom nothing. Devising figments to temper his nothingness. Quick leave him. Pause and again in panic to himself, Quick leave him.

Devised deviser devising it all for company. In the same figment dark as his figments. In what posture and if or not as hearer in his for good not yet devised. Is not one immovable enough? Why duplicate this particular solace? Then let him move. Within reason. On all fours. A moderate crawl torso well clear of the ground eyes front alert. If this no better than nothing cancel. If possible. And in the void regained another motion. Or none. Leaving only the most helpful posture to be devised. But to be going on with let him crawl. Crawl and fall. Crawl again and fall again. In the same figment dark as his other figments.

From ranging far and wide as if in quest the voice comes to rest and constant faintness. To rest where? Imagine warily.

Above the upturned face. Falling tangent to the crown. So that in the faint light it sheds were there a mouth to be seen he would not see it. Roll as he might his eyes. Height from the ground?

Arm's length. Force? Low. A mother's stooping over cradle from behind. She moves aside to let the father look. In his turn he murmurs to the newborn. Flat tone unchanged. No trace of love.

You are on your back at the foot of an aspen. In its trembling shade. She at right angles propped on her elbows head between her hands. Your eyes opened and closed have looked in hers looking in yours. In your dark you look in them again. Still. You feel on your face the fringe of her long black hair stirring in the still air. Within the tent of hair your faces are hidden from view. She murmurs, Listen to the leaves. Eyes in each other's eyes you listen to the leaves. In their trembling shade.

Crawling and falling then. Crawling again and falling again. If this finally no improvement on nothing he can always fall for good. Or have never risen to his knees. Contrive how such crawl unlike the voice may serve to chart the area. However roughly. First what is the unit of crawl? Corresponding to the footstep of erect locomotion. He rises to all fours and makes ready to set out. Hands and knees angles of an oblong two foot long width irrelevant. Finally say left knee moves forward six inches thus half halving distance between it and homologous hand. Which then in due course in its turn moves forward by as much. Oblong now rhomboid. But for no longer than it takes right knee and hand to follow suit. Oblong restored. So on till he drops. Of all modes of crawl this the repent amble is possibly the least common. And so possibly of all the most diverting.

So as he crawls the mute count. Grain by grain in the mind. One two three four one. Knee hand knee hand two. One foot. Till say after five he falls. Then sooner or later on from nought anew. One two three four one. Knee hand knee hand two. Six. So on. In what he wills a beeline. Till having encountered no obstacle discouraged he heads back the way he came. From nought anew. Or in some quite different direction. In what he hopes a beeline. Till again with no dead end for his pains he renounces and embarks on yet another course. From nought anew. Well aware or little doubting how darkness may deflect. Withershins on account of the heart. Or conversely to shortest path convert deliberate veer. Be that as it may and crawl as he will no bourne as yet. As yet imaginable. Hand knee hand knee as he will. Bourneless dark.

Would it be reasonable to imagine the hearer as mentally quite inert? Except when he hears. That is when the voice sounds. For what if not it and his breath is there for him to hear? Aha! The crawl. Does he hear the crawl? The fall? What an addition to company were he but to hear the crawl. The fall. The rising to all fours again. The crawl resumed. And wonder to himself what in the world such sounds might signify. Reserve for a duller moment. What if not sound could set his mind in motion? Sight? The temptation is strong to decree there is nothing to see. But too late for the moment. For he sees a change of dark when he opens or shuts his eyes. And he may see the faint light the voice imagined to shed. Rashly imagined. Light infinitely faint it is true since now no more than a mere murmur. Here suddenly seen how his eyes close as soon as the voice sounds. Should they happen to be open at the time. So light as let be faintest light no longer perceived than the time it takes the lid to fall. Taste? The taste in his mouth? Long since dulled. Touch? The thrust of the ground against his bones. All the way from calcaneum to bump of philogenitiveness. Might not a notion to stir ruffle his apathy? To turn on his side. On his face. For a change. Let that much of want be conceded. With attendant relief that the days are no more when he could writhe in vain. Smell? His own? Long since dulled. And a barrier to others if any. Such as might have once emitted a rat long dead. Or some other carrion. Yet to be imagined. Unless the crawler smell. Aha! The crawling creator. Might the crawling creator be reasonably imagined

to smell? Even fouler than his creature.
Stirring now and then to wonder that
mind so lost to wonder. To wonder what
in the world can be making that alien
smell. Whence in the world those wafts of
villainous smell. How much more companionable could his creator but smell.
Could he but smell his creator. Some sixth
sense? Inexplicable premonition of impending ill? Yes or no? No. Pure reason?
Beyond experience. God is love. Yes or
no? No.

Can the crawling creator
crawling in the same create dark as his
creature create while crawling? One of the
questions he put to himself as between
two crawls he lay. And if the obvious answer were not far to seek the most helpful
was another matter. And many crawls
were necessary and the like number of
prostrations before he could finally make
up his imagination on this score. Adding
to himself without conviction in the same

breath as always that no answer of his was
sacred. Come what might the answer he
hazarded in the end was no he could not.
Crawling in the dark in the way described
was too serious a matter and too all-en-
grossing to permit of any other business
were it only the conjuring of something
out of nothing. For he had not only as
perhaps too hastily imagined to cover the
ground in this special way but rectigrade
into the bargain to the best of his ability.
And furthermore to count as he went adding half foot to half foot and retain in his
memory the ever-changing sum of those
gone before. And finally to maintain eyes
and ears at a high level of alertness for any
clue however small to the nature of the
place to which imagination perhaps unad-
visedly had consigned him. So while in
the same breath deploring a fancy so reason-ridden and observing how revocable
its flights he could not but answer finally
no he could not. Could not conceivably
create while crawling in the same create
dark as his creature.

A strand. Evening. Light dying. Soon none left to die. No. No such thing then as no light. Died on to dawn and never died. You stand with your back to the wash. No sound but its. Ever fainter as it slowly ebbs. Till it slowly flows again. You lean on a long staff. Your hands rest on the knob and on them your head. Were your eyes to open they would first see far below in the last rays the skirt of your greatcoat and the uppers of your boots emerging from the sand. Then and it alone till it vanishes the shadow of the staff on the sand. Vanishes from your sight. Moonless starless night. Were your eyes to open dark would lighten.

Crawls and falls. Lies. Lies in the dark with closed eyes resting from his crawl. Recovering. Physically and from his disappointment at having crawled again in vain. Perhaps saying to himself, Why crawl at all? Why not just lie in the dark with closed eyes and give up? Give up all. Have done with all. With bootless crawl and figments comfortless. But if on occasion so disheartened it is seldom for long. For little by little as he lies the craving for company revives. In which to escape from his own. The need to hear that voice again. If only saying again, You are on your back in the dark. Or if only, You first saw the light and cried at the close of the day when in darkness Christ at the ninth hour cried and died. The need eyes closed the better to hear to see that glimmer shed. Or with addition of some human weakness to improve the hearer. For example an itch beyond reach of the hand or better still within while the hand immovable. An unscratchable itch. What an addition to company that would be! Or last if not least resort to ask himself what precisely he means when he speaks of himself loosely as lying. Which in other words of all the innumerable ways of lying is likely to prove in the long run the most endearing. If having crawled in the way described he falls it would normally be on his face. Indeed given the degree of his fatigue and discouragement at this point it is hard to see how he could do otherwise. But once fallen and lying on his face there is no reason why he should not turn over on one or other of his sides or on his only back and so lie should any of these three postures offer better company than any of the other three. The supine though most tempting he must finally disallow as being already supplied by the hearer. With regard to the sidelong one glance is enough to dispel them both. Leaving him with no other choice than the prone. But how prone? Prone how? How disposed the legs? The arms? The head? Prone in the dark he strains to see how best he may lie prone. How most companionably.

See hearer clearer. Which of all the ways of lying supine the least likely in the long run to pall? After long straining eyes closed prone in the dark the following. But first naked or covered? If only with a sheet. Naked. Ghostly in the voice's glimmer that bonewhite flesh for company. Head resting mainly on occipital bump aforesaid. Legs joined at attention. Feet splayed ninety degrees. Hands invisibly manacled crossed on pubis. Other details as need felt. Leave him at that for the moment.

Numb with the woes of your kind you raise none the less your head from off your hands and open your eyes. You turn on without moving from your place the light above you. Your eyes light on the watch lying beneath it. But instead of reading the hour of night they follow round and round the second hand now followed and now preceded by its shadow. Hours later it seems to you as follows. At 60 seconds and 30 seconds shadow hidden by hand. From 60 to 30 shadow precedes hand at a distance increasing from zero at 60 to maximum at

15 and thence decreasing to new zero at
30. From 30 to 60 shadow follows hand
at a distance increasing from zero at 30 to
maximum at 45 and thence decreasing to
new zero at 60. Slant light now to dial by
moving either to either side and hand
hides shadow at two quite different points
as for example 50 and 20. Indeed at any
two quite different points whatever de-
pending on degree of slant. But however
great or small the slant and more or less
remote from initial 60 and 30 the new
points of zero shadow the space between
the two remains one of 30 seconds. The
shadow emerges from under hand at any
point whatever of its circuit to follow or
precede it for the space of 30 seconds.
Then disappears infinitely briefly before
emerging again to precede or follow it for
the space of 30 seconds again. And so on
and on. This would seem to be the one
constant. For the very distance itself between hand and shadow varies as the degree of slant. But however great or small
this distance it invariably waxes and wanes

from nothing to a maximum 15 seconds later and to nothing again 15 seconds later again respectively. And so on and on. This would seem to be a second constant. More might have been observed on the subject of this second hand and its shadow in their seemingly endless parallel rotation round and round the dial and other variables and constants brought to light and errors if any corrected in what had seemed so far. But unable to continue you bow your head back to where it was and with closed eyes return to the woes of your kind. Dawn finds you still in this position. The low sun shines on you through the eastern window and flings all along the floor your shadow and that of the lamp left lit above you. And those of other objects also.

What visions in the dark of light! Who exclaims thus? Who asks who exclaims, What visions in the shadeless dark of light and shade! Yet another still? Devising it all for company. What a further addition to company that would be! Yet another still devising it all for company. Quick leave him.

Somehow at any price to make an end when you could go out no more you sat huddled in the dark. Having covered in your day some twenty-five thousand leagues or roughly thrice the girdle. And never once overstepped a radius of one from home. Home! So sat waiting to be purged the old lutist cause of Dante's first quarter-smile and now perhaps singing praises with some section of the blest at last. To whom here in any case farewell. The place is windowless. When as you sometimes do to void the fluid you open your eyes dark lessens. Thus you now on your back in the dark once sat huddled there your body having shown you it could go out no more. Out no more to walk the little winding back roads and interjacent pastures now alive with flocks and now deserted. With at your elbow for long years your father's shade in his old tramping rags and then for long years alone. Adding step after step to the ever mounting sum of those already accomplished. Halting now and then with bowed head to fix the score. Then on from nought anew. Huddled thus you find yourself imagining you are not alone while knowing full well that nothing has occurred to make this possible. The process continues none the less lapped as it were in its meaninglessness. You do not murmur in so many words, I know this doomed to fail and yet persist. No. For the first personal singular and a fortiori plural pronoun had never any place in your vocabulary. But without a word you view yourself to this effect as you would a stranger suffering say from Hodgkin's disease or if you prefer Percival Pott's surprised at prayer. From time to time with unexpected grace you lie. Simultaneously

the various parts set out. The arms un-
clasp the knees. The head lifts. The legs
start to straighten. The trunk tilts back-
ward. And together these and countless
others continue on their respective ways
till they can go no further and together
come to rest. Supine now you resume
your fable where the act of lying cut it
short. And persist till the converse opera-
tion cuts it short again. So in the dark
now huddled and now supine you toil in
vain. And just as from the former position
to the latter the shift grows easier in time
and more alacrious so from the latter to
the former the reverse is true. Till from
the occasional relief it was supineness be-
comes habitual and finally the rule. You
now on your back in the dark shall not
rise to your arse again to clasp your legs in
your arms and bow down your head till it
can bow down no further. But with face
upturned for good labour in vain at your
fable. Till finally you hear how words are
coming to an end. With every inane word
a little nearer to the last. And how the

fable too. The fable of one with you in the dark. The fable of one fabling of one with you in the dark. And how better in the end labour lost and silence. And you as you always were.

Alone.